EAGLE FEATHER

"*I will pay you what it costs to have your truck fixed,*" said Father.

"*It will take half your sheep and goats,*" said Crook Nose. "*Maybe more.*"

Father said nothing. He looked at Eagle Feather. Eagle Feather did not know what to say.

"*But you are a poor man,*" said Crook Nose. "*I will make it easy for you.*"

"*How?*" asked Father.

"*Let your son work for me this summer,*" said Crook Nose. "*That will pay for fixing the truck.*"

"Following an unthinking act, Eagle Feather must work all summer for a crafty cousin, but he looks forward to school in the fall. When his cousin refuses to let him go to school, Eagle Feather runs away. Told simply and sympathetically, this story gives a good picture of Navajo Indian life. Three songs are included." —*Library Journal*

"This story has authentic atmosphere and character study." —*Kirkus Reviews*

WITHDRAWN

CHARLOTTE E. HOBBS
MEMORIAL LIBRARY
LOVELL, ME 04051

EAGLE
FEATHER

BY CLYDE ROBERT BULLA

Illustrated by Tom Two Arrows

SCHOLASTIC INC.
New York Toronto London Auckland Sydney

No part of this publication may be reproduced in whole or in part, or stored in a retrieval system, or transmitted in any form, or by any means, electronic, mechanical, photocopying, recording, or otherwise, without written permission of the publisher. For information regarding permission, write to Puffin Books, a division of Penguin Books USA Inc., 375 Hudson Street, New York, NY 10014.

ISBN 0-590-26270-X

Copyright © 1953 by Clyde Robert Bulla. Copyright renewed 1981 by Clyde Robert Bulla. All rights reserved. Published by Scholastic Inc., 555 Broadway, New York, NY 10012, by arrangement with Puffin Books, a division of Penguin Books USA Inc.

12 11 10 9 8 7 6 5 4 3   5 6 7 8 9/9 0/0

Printed in the U.S.A.   40

First Scholastic printing, February 1995

To

Elizabeth Riley

CONTENTS

MY HOGAN *

In an even rhythm

mf

In my ho-gan— May there ev-er be peace— and joy.— In my ho-gan— may plen-ty ev-er be.— May the winds blow soft-ly.— May the great sun look down kind-ly.— May the moon shine gent-ly— On my ho-gan.—

* Pronounced ho-GAHN.

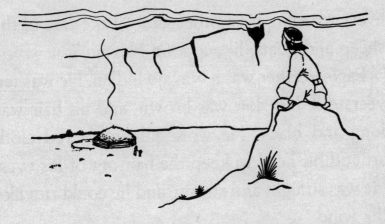

I IN THE HOGAN

Eagle Feather sang as he drove the sheep and goats down the trail. He was glad it was evening and time to go home.

Every morning he took the sheep and goats to pasture. He took them where they could find good grass and leaves to eat. He kept them from getting lost.

He worked hard to care for them, because

1

every morning his mother said, "Take care of the sheep and goats, like a good Navajo."

Eagle Feather was a Navajo Indian. He was ten years old. His skin was brown, and his hair was long and black. He wore a band of red cloth around his head to keep the hair out of his eyes. He was straight and strong, and he could run like the wind.

"Hi!" he said to the sheep and goats. He ran after them to make them go faster.

Down in the valley he could see his little brother and sister. Their names were Teasing Boy and Morning Bird. They were waiting for him by the corral.

"Open the gate!" he called.

They opened the gate. He drove the sheep and goats into the corral, and they were safe for the night.

Teasing Boy was jumping about like a goat. He was glad to see his brother, but he liked to tease him, too. "A man came here while you were gone," he said.

"What man?" asked Eagle Feather.

"A big man," said Teasing Boy. "He rode a yellow horse. He talked to Mother. I think he wants you to go to school."

Eagle Feather asked his sister, "Did a man come here?"

"Yes," said Morning Bird.

"I won't go to school," said Eagle Feather.

Teasing Boy and Morning Bird looked at each other behind Eagle Feather's back. They put their hands over their mouths to keep from laughing out loud.

"He can't make me go to school!" said Eagle Feather.

3

"The man is here now," said Teasing Boy.

Eagle Feather looked toward the hogan, the house where the family lived. It was a small house with only one room. It was made of logs and covered with earth. From the outside it looked like a little round hill.

"I'm not going in there," he said. "I don't want to see that man."

"He won't hurt you," said Morning Bird. "Mother wants you to see him."

Mother came to the door of the hogan. She had on the green jacket and long, brown skirt that Eagle Feather liked so well. He liked to touch the jacket. It was soft as fur, and there were silver buttons on it. Around her skirt were bright bands of yellow and red.

"Come!" she called. "Time for supper."

Teasing Boy and Morning Bird took hold of

4

Eagle Feather's arms. He let them pull him into
the hogan. There was a fire in the circle of stones
on the floor. The smoke went up through the hole
in the top of the hogan.

A man was sitting by the fire.

Eagle Feather stood still.

"Father!" he said.

Teasing Boy and Morning Bird were laughing.
"We played a joke on our brother," said Teasing

5

Boy. "We told him a man was here. We didn't say who it was."

Father had been away a day and a night. He had gone to trade one of his old horses for a better one.

Eagle Feather sat down by him. "Did you trade the horse?"

"Yes," said Father. "I had to give a saddle, besides. Now I have a good yellow horse. He is tied out under the trees."

"They told me a man was here and he wanted me to go to school," said Eagle Feather. "When they said that, I didn't want to come in."

"School might be a good thing," said Father. "Don't you ever want to go?"

"No," said Eagle Feather. "I want to stay here. I want to take care of the sheep and goats and ride the horses. I don't want to go to any school."

Mother took the kettle off the fire.

"Eat," she said.

Everyone dipped into the kettle and took out pieces of meat. They had big, round pieces of soft bread to eat with the meat.

While they ate, the fire began to die. Soon the hogan was almost dark.

Morning Bird asked her father, "Will you sing a song?"

He sang a song about the hogan.

"Now will you tell stories?" asked Eagle Feather.

Father told a story about wonderful people who made the rain and rode on rainbows and flew with the wind.

"I could listen to stories all night!" said Eagle Feather. "Will you tell another one?"

"It is time to sleep now," said Father. "I have to be up early in the morning."

"Are you going away again?" asked Eagle Feather.

"Yes. To the trading post," said Father.

"Are you going to trade the fine new rug

8

our mother has made?" asked Morning Bird.

"Yes," said Father. "I will trade it for flour."

"I need more things, too," said Mother. "I need sugar and coffee and some cans of pork and beans."

"Then I will take two horses," said Father.

"Let me ride one," said Eagle Feather.

"Do you want to go to the trading post with me?" asked Father.

"Yes!" said Eagle Feather.

Father looked at Mother. "Our son has been to the trading post only once. He was a baby then, and he cannot remember it. It might be good for him to go again."

"Yes," said Mother. "He can go, I think."

"I want to go, too," said Teasing Boy.

"No. You must stay and take care of the sheep and goats," said Mother.

9

It was time to go to bed.

Father and Teasing Boy and Eagle Feather lay down on one side of the hogan. Mother and Morning Bird lay down on the other side. They all slept on sheepskins.

It was hard for Eagle Feather to go to sleep. He kept looking at the stars through the smoke-hole over his head. He kept thinking, "Tomorrow I go to the trading post with Father. Tomorrow—tomorrow!"

II ON THE TRAIL

Early in the morning Eagle Feather and his father rode away. Teasing Boy and Morning Bird were still asleep. Mother stood outside the hogan and watched as they rode off down the trail. The two dogs, Old Black and Slick Dog, wanted to go. They ran behind the horses, but Father drove them back.

"We are going so far, they might get lost," he said.

Father was riding his yellow horse. Eagle Feather rode the spotted pony.

Father had on his wide black hat and blue shirt. He had silver rings in his ears. The rings were set with blue stones. Eagle Feather thought he looked very fine.

11

Eagle Feather wore his red headband. He had a red handkerchief around his neck. He wore blue jeans and a sheepskin jacket.

He told his father, "I don't need my jacket."

"You will at night," said his father. "It gets cold then."

"Are we going to stay all night at the trading post?" asked Eagle Feather.

"Yes," said Father. "It will take nearly all day to get there. We will go home tomorrow."

Mother's rug was rolled up and tied to Father's saddle. Eagle Feather had watched her weave it on the loom. It was red, black, and gray, made of wool from their sheep. It had taken her a long time to weave it.

"How much will you get for the rug?" asked Eagle Feather.

"I don't know," said Father. "It is not very big."

"But it is pretty," said Eagle Feather. "It has big lightning in the middle and little lightning at both ends."

They rode along side by side. Sometimes Father sang. Eagle Feather sang with him. He was glad it was spring and the air was clear and bright. He was glad the red cactus flowers were

13

in bloom. Most of all, he was glad he was going to the trading post with his father.

They rode up a steep trail that led through pine trees and over rocks. The trail was so steep the horses had to go in a slow walk.

Now Father was riding ahead.

Eagle Feather called to him, "I heard something move in the bushes."

"Where?" asked Father.

"Back there," said Eagle Feather.

"I don't see anything," said Father.

Eagle Feather heard the sound again. He looked back. He saw the bushes move.

"Something is coming after us," he said.

Father stopped and looked back. This time he saw the bushes move.

Eagle Feather had his bow and arrows. He took his bow off the saddle horn. He took an arrow out of his saddle pocket. "It may be a wolf," he said. "It may be a bear."

All at once Father began to laugh. The bushes moved again. Two dogs ran out into the trail.

"Look!" said Eagle Feather. "Slick Dog and Old Black!"

"They followed us," said Father.

"They wanted to go to the trading post, too," said Eagle Feather.

"We will let them come with us," said Father. "It is too far to take them home."

They rode on up the trail. Slick Dog and Old Black ran beside them.

"Are you hungry?" asked Father.

"Yes," said Eagle Feather.

They stopped under a tree and tied the horses where they could eat grass. Father had a roll of dried meat in his pocket. He gave some to Eagle

15

Feather and ate some himself. They drank from the water bottle. Then they were ready to go again.

They rode until late in the day. The trail was not so steep now.

"We will soon be there," said Father. "See those big cottonwood trees?"

"I see them," said Eagle Feather.

"Under those cottonwood trees is the trading post," said Father.

"I can see it," said Eagle Feather.

He could see a big stone house. He could see horses tied under the trees. There were wagons under the trees, too, and there was one truck. Near the trading post were many people. Most of them were Indians. A few were white.

Eagle Feather began to feel shy. He always felt shy with strange people. He kept close to his father as they rode up to the trading post.

III THE TRADING POST

Eagle Feather and his father went inside the trading post. Eagle Feather looked all around the big, cool room. There were shelves on all sides. On the shelves were shirts and blue jeans and jackets and hats. There were blankets and boots and knives and belts.

He saw cans of fruit and cans of pork and beans. He could not read the words on the cans, but he knew by the pictures what was inside.

He saw candy in a glass case. There were candy bars and gumdrops and hard candy.

Father talked to Mr. Neal, the trader. Mr. Neal was a white man. Father showed him the rug.

Eagle Feather looked at the candy. He hoped his father would buy him some.

A man spoke to him. "Hello."

Eagle Feather was so shy he did not look up.

"Do you want to buy some candy?" asked the man. "I will sell you some."

"I want to look first," said Eagle Feather.

"All right," said the man.

Eagle Feather looked up at him. The man was a young Navajo, but his hair was cut short like a white man's. He had a friendly smile. Eagle Feather liked him.

"Do you work here?" he asked.

"Yes," said the man. "I'm Jimmie Redhorse. I know your father."

Eagle Feather's father came over to the candy case. "Give my son a bottle of pop," he said.

"What kind?" asked Jimmie. "Strawberry, orange, or grape?"

Father asked Eagle Feather, "What kind?"

"Orange," said Eagle Feather.

Jimmie gave him the bottle of pop, and Father paid for it.

Eagle Feather went out under the trees to drink his pop. It was cold and good. He wished he could take some to his brother and sister.

Three other Indian boys were sitting under the trees.

One of them asked Eagle Feather, "Where do you come from?"

Eagle Feather pointed to the west.

"I come from the south," said the boy.

"From across the canyon?" asked Eagle Feather.

"Yes," said the boy. "Far across the canyon."

Jimmie Redhorse came out and sat down by Eagle Feather. "Do you boys want to have a race?" he asked.

"A horse race?" asked Eagle Feather.

"No. A foot race. Do you want to line up there and see how fast you can run?"

The other boys lined up. Eagle Feather lined up with them.

The men and women outside the trading post saw there was going to be a race. They came up to watch.

"See the big red rock over there?" asked Jimmie. "Run to the rock and back here to this cottonwood tree. Ready? *Go!*"

Two of the boys were bigger than Eagle Feather. "They can run faster than I can," he thought. But he ran as fast as he could.

He was the first one to the rock. And back at the cottonwood tree, he was far ahead of all the others.

"Did you see him run!" said a woman to Eagle Feather's father. "His name should be Running Boy."

"We call him Eagle Feather," said Father. "When he was only a baby he liked to go hunting on the hill by our hogan. One day he

22

brought home an eagle feather he had found. That is why we call him Eagle Feather."

Jimmie gave Eagle Feather a sack of hard candy.

"This is your prize," he said, "because you won the race."

They sat under the trees.

23

"You can run fast," said Jimmie. "Do you like games? Do you like to play baseball?"

"I don't know how," said Eagle Feather.

"Didn't you learn in school?" asked Jimmie.

"I never went to school," said Eagle Feather.

"Why not?" asked Jimmie.

"I don't want to go. I want to be at home with my father and mother and my brother and sister," said Eagle Feather. "At school they shut you up in rooms all the time. They make you do things you don't want to do. They whip you with big sticks."

"Who told you that?" asked Jimmie.

"I heard a man say it."

"They didn't do things like that to me." Jimmie got up. "Come on. Let me show you where I went to school."

"Where is it?" asked Eagle Feather.

"Here at the trading post. Just over the hill."
Eagle Feather hung back.

"Come on," said Jimmie. "There's nothing to
be afraid of."

Eagle Feather went with him. From the top of
the hill he could see the schoolhouse. It was a
long building made of stone. There was a small
stone house near it.

"This is vacation time," said Jimmie. "No one
is here but the teacher. She lives in the small
house."

He knocked at the teacher's door. A white
woman came out.

25

"Hello, Mrs. Mack," said Jimmie. "I have a friend with me. I want to show him the school."

"All right, Jimmie," said Mrs. Mack. "Here is the key."

Jimmie took the key and opened the schoolhouse door. He went in. Eagle Feather went in after him. He walked very slowly, and he felt very strange. It was the first time he had ever been inside a schoolhouse.

Jimmie showed him the two big rooms where the boys and girls slept at night. He showed him the kitchen. It was clean, and the walls were white.

"Two Navajo women cook here for the boys and girls," Jimmie said. "The next room is where the boys and girls eat. The last room is where they study and have their classes."

Eagle Feather looked at the classroom. He

26

looked at the seats and desks. He looked at the pictures on the walls. There were pictures of trees and hogans and horses and saddles.

"Who made these?" he asked.

"The boys and girls," said Jimmie. "In school they learn to draw and paint."

Eagle Feather looked at the shelves of books. "Do these books have stories in them?"

"Yes," said Jimmie. "Do you like stories?"

"I like the ones my father tells," said Eagle Feather.

"If you went to school, you would learn to read," said Jimmie. "You could read all the stories in these books."

Eagle Feather said nothing.

Jimmie took him out into the schoolyard. "This is where the boys and girls play."

By that time the sun was down. Jimmie took

27

the schoolhouse key back to the teacher. He and Eagle Feather walked back to the trading post.

Eagle Feather went with his father.

"I sold the rug," said Father. "The trader gave me a good price for it."

"That is good," said Eagle Feather.

They built a fire beside a rock and made coffee in a can. They drank coffee and ate dried meat. Then they rolled up in their blankets and lay down to sleep.

The moon and stars were bright. The night was almost as bright as day.

Father looked at Eagle Feather. "Your eyes are open," he said. "Can't you go to sleep?"

"I am thinking," said Eagle Feather.

"What are you thinking?" asked Father.

Eagle Feather said, "I am thinking about that school."

IV CROOK NOSE

Eagle Feather was driving the sheep and goats home from pasture. It was a week since he had come back from the trading post. He still thought of the things he had seen there. Most of all, he thought of the school and the books full of stories.

Teasing Boy and Morning Bird were waiting by the corral.

29

"Come to the hogan," said Teasing Boy. "Father wants you."

"You can't play another joke on me," said Eagle Feather. "Father isn't here."

"Yes, he is," said Morning Bird.

"No," said Eagle Feather. "He went to a sing. Sam Gray Bear's little girl is sick, and a medicine man is singing over her to make her well."

"Father came home from the sing," said Teasing Boy. "A man came with him. The man came in a truck."

"He is our cousin Crook Nose," said Morning Bird.

"That is just a story, I think," said Eagle Feather.

He drove the sheep and goats into the corral and shut the gate. He started up toward the hogan. And there behind the hogan was a truck!

30

"Now do you believe me?" said Teasing Boy.

Father came to the door of the hogan. "Come in," he said to Eagle Feather. He said to Teasing Boy and Morning Bird, "Play outside."

Eagle Feather went inside. A man was there with Father and Mother. He had sharp eyes and a crooked nose.

He smiled at Eagle Feather. "Do you know me? I am your cousin."

"Yes, I know you," said Eagle Feather.

He sat down on the floor. They all sat and looked at one another.

Crook Nose said to Father, "He looks like a strong boy."

"Yes," said Father.

"At the trading post they say he is strong and can run very fast," said Crook Nose.

"That is true," said Father.

"And he takes good care of the sheep and goats?" said Crook Nose.

"Yes," said Father.

"Of course, he is just a boy," said Crook Nose.

32

"I could not give him a man's pay. But I will see that he has money to spend."

Eagle Feather whispered to his mother, "What are they talking about?"

"Your cousin has a boy and a girl, but they are small," said Mother. "He needs a boy who can take care of his sheep and goats. He wants you to go and live with him for a while."

"Do I have to go?" asked Eagle Feather.

"No," said Mother.

"It is for you to decide," said Father.

"But I need you more than they do," said Crook Nose. "They have your brother and sister to help them. My boy and girl are not big enough to help me." He smiled at Eagle Feather. "We will have good times together. I will take you to town in my truck. You can spend the money I will pay you."

33

"Can I go to school?" asked Eagle Feather.

"School? Yes!" said Crook Nose. "In the fall I will send you to school."

Eagle Feather did not know what to say.

"Don't make up your mind now," said Mother. "Think about it a while."

"All right," said Eagle Feather.

He went outside. He sat down on a rock.

Teasing Boy and Morning Bird came up and pulled at his arms. "Let's go slide down the bank!" they said.

"Go away," said Eagle Feather. "I have to think."

After a while they left him alone.

He sat and looked at the sky. The sun looked like a big, red ball as it went down behind the cliffs. A little wind blew through the pines and sagebrush. He could smell the wood smoke from

the hogan. He could hear Teasing Boy and Morning Bird laughing as they slid down the bank.

The two dogs came up to him. They looked surprised to see him so quiet. They lay down close to him.

All the time he sat there, he was thinking.

35

When the sky began to grow dark, he got up and went into the hogan.

"Have you made up your mind?" asked Mother.

"Yes," said Eagle Feather.

"And you are going back with me in the morning?" asked Crook Nose.

"No," said Eagle Feather. "I am going to stay here."

V CROOK NOSE'S TRUCK

Crook Nose stayed all night in the hogan. In the morning Mother went to milk the goats. Crook Nose and Father went to the corral with her.

Crook Nose's truck was on a little hill back of the hogan. Teasing Boy and Morning Bird went to look at it. They had not seen many cars before. The road was so rough that not many cars had ever been there.

"I wish I could ride in it," said Morning Bird.

"I wish I could make it go," said Teasing Boy.

Eagle Feather came out of the hogan.

Morning Bird called to him, "Come and look at this big truck."

"It is not so big," said Eagle Feather. "I saw bigger ones at the trading post."

37

"I want to get in." Morning Bird tried to climb through the window, but her long skirt caught on the door.

"How do you open the door?" asked Teasing Boy.

Eagle Feather opened the door.

"Show us how to drive," said Teasing Boy. "Show us how to drive the truck!"

Eagle Feather got in. Teasing Boy and Morning Bird got in beside him.

"You take hold of the wheel—like this," said Eagle Feather. "If you want to go north, you turn the wheel to the north."

"What are all the things down here?" asked Teasing Boy.

"Those are things you work with your feet," said Eagle Feather.

"What is the stick that comes out of the floor?" asked Teasing Boy.

"I think they call it the brake," said Eagle Feather.

"What is it for?" asked Teasing Boy.

"I don't know," said Eagle Feather.

"Does it move?" asked Teasing Boy. "Let me

see." He slid to the floor of the truck. He pushed and pulled at the brake.

"Don't do that," said Eagle Feather. He tried to pull Teasing Boy's hands off the brake. "Let go!"

"No!" said Teasing Boy.

They began to fight. Just then the brake moved. The truck began to move.

"I want to get out!" said Morning Bird. She tried to open the door.

The truck was rolling down the hill. Eagle Feather held on to the wheel. He could see nothing but rocks and trees ahead. Teasing Boy jumped up into the seat. He and Morning Bird bumped their heads together.

The truck ran over a rock and almost tipped over. It ran into a small pine tree and stopped. The door flew open.

Eagle Feather got out.

Father and Crook Nose were running toward him. Morning Bird and Teasing Boy were out of the truck and running toward the hogan.

41

"My truck!" cried Crook Nose. "Look at my truck!"

He got into it. He backed it over the rocks and into the road.

"It still runs," said Father.

"Yes, but one light is broken. The wheels are crooked, too." Crook Nose got out and looked at the truck and shook his head.

"The wheels were crooked before, I think," said Father.

"Not like this," said Crook Nose. "I will have to take it to town to have it fixed. It will cost more money than you make all summer."

Father said to Eagle Feather, "What do you have to say?"

"We were in the truck," said Eagle Feather. "We had a fight over the brake, and the truck went down the hill."

"Why were you in the truck?" asked Father.

"I don't know," said Eagle Feather.

"Who opened the door?" asked Father.

"I did," said Eagle Feather.

"Who was the first one in?"

"I was," said Eagle Feather.

"Then you are to blame," said Father. "You are the oldest. You should have known better."

"Yes, he is to blame," said Crook Nose.

"I will pay you what it costs to have your truck fixed," said Father.

"It will take half your sheep and goats," said Crook Nose. "Maybe more."

Father said nothing. He looked at Eagle Feather. Eagle Feather did not know what to say.

"But you are a poor man," said Crook Nose. "I will make it easy for you."

"How?" asked Father.

"Let your son work for me this summer," said Crook Nose. "That will pay for fixing the truck."

Father asked Eagle Feather, "What do you say?"

Crook Nose began to smile. There was something about his smile that Eagle Feather did not like. "I—I want to think about it," he said.

"Yes, think about it," said Father. "You don't have to go if you don't want to."

Eagle Feather took the sheep and goats to pasture. All day he thought. He knew that Father was a poor man. Sometimes in the winter they did not have enough to eat. "If Crook Nose takes half our sheep and goats," he said to himself, "we will not have enough to live on all year."

Then he said to himself, "I am to blame. I should not have got into the truck. I should have kept my brother and sister out, too."

In the evening, when he drove the sheep and goats home, Crook Nose and Father were sitting by the hogan.

Eagle Feather went up to them. He said to Crook Nose, "I will work for you this summer."

VI FAR FROM HOME

It was a long way to Crook Nose's hogan. It took half a day to drive there in the truck. Eagle Feather had never been so far from home before.

All around the hogan he saw sheep and goats. In front of the hogan he saw Crook Nose's wife, Round Woman. She had a baby girl on her back. The baby was tied to her cradle board.

Eagle Feather got out of the truck.

46

"Here is your box," said Crook Nose.

Eagle Feather took the box he had brought from home.

Round Woman asked, "Is this the boy?"

"Yes," said Crook Nose. "See how big he is? He is strong, too. He knows how to take care of sheep and goats."

"That is good," said Round Woman. "He can take them to pasture. I have too much to do to watch them all day." She asked Eagle Feather, "What is in that box?"

"My clothes," he said.

"Put them inside."

He went into the hogan. There were sheep-skins on the floor. A boy was sitting on the floor.

When he saw Eagle Feather, he jumped up and hid under the sheepskins. Eagle Feather put down the box and went outside.

"Is that your boy in the hogan?" he asked.

"Yes, that is Small Boy," said Crook Nose. "He is too small to take care of the sheep and goats. Come with me now, and I will show you what to do."

He showed Eagle Feather how many sheep and goats there were. He told him where to take them to pasture. He told him how to find the water hole.

"Before I go, let me get my bow and arrow," said Eagle Feather.

He went to the hogan. At first he could not find the box he had brought from home. Then he saw it, upside down. Everything had been taken out of it and thrown about the hogan. His shirt and jeans were lying in the dirt.

Small Boy looked out from under the sheepskins.

"Did you do this?" Eagle Feather asked him.

Round Woman came into the hogan. "Yes, he did it." She laughed as if she thought it was funny.

Eagle Feather did not think it was funny. He picked up his clothes and put them back into the box.

"Where can I put this," he asked, "so he can't get into it again?"

"He won't hurt your things," said Round Woman. She was still laughing. Small Boy came out from under the sheepskins and began to laugh, too.

Crook Nose came to the door. "Come," he said. "Take the sheep and goats to pasture."

So Eagle Feather's work began.

Every day he cared for the sheep and goats. In the morning and evening he worked for Round

49

Woman. He cut wood and carried it to the hogan. He carried water, too. He hoed in the garden. He milked the goats.

Crook Nose was gone most of the time. He hauled things in the truck. Sometimes he hauled sheep and goats to town and sold them. He went to sings and dances.

Eagle Feather did not like to work for Round Woman. Her tongue was sharp and she often scolded him.

"You are the slowest boy I ever saw," she said. "Why can't you work faster!"

He was glad to be away from her. He was glad when it was time to take the sheep and goats to pasture.

He liked to sit on a high place where he could see all the sheep and goats. Sometimes he sang to them:

Eat the good grass, little sheep,
Eat the good grass, little goats,
While I watch over you.
Pinyon pine needles will make you sick.
I will not let you eat them.
Loco weeds will make you crazy.
I will not let you eat them.
No coyote will harm you
And none of you will be lost.
Eat the good grass
While I watch over you.

One day he was watching the sheep and goats not far from the hogan. Small Boy came out of the bushes.

"I am going to ride the old black goat," he said.

"The black goat will throw you off and hurt you," said Eagle Feather.

"No," said Small Boy. He caught the black goat around the neck and jumped on his back. The goat began to run. Small Boy fell off. He was not hurt, but he had torn a hole in the leg of his jeans.

"You are making the sheep and goats afraid," said Eagle Feather. "Go back to the hogan."

Small Boy pointed his finger at Eagle Feather.

"Don't do that," said Eagle Feather. "Don't you know it is bad to point at someone?"

Small Boy kept on pointing his finger. Eagle Feather turned his head so he could not see him.

Something hit him in the back of the head. It was a hard piece of dirt that Small Boy had thrown.

"I'll get you!" shouted Eagle Feather.

Small Boy turned and ran. Eagle Feather ran after him.

53

In front of the hogan, Small Boy fell down. He began to cry.

Round Woman came out of the hogan. "What did you do to my son!" She picked up a stick and struck Eagle Feather with it. "Go back to your work and leave my son alone!"

Eagle Feather went back to the sheep and goats. His head hurt where Small Boy had struck him with the piece of dirt. His arm hurt where Round Woman had struck him with the stick.

He wished he could go home.

He missed his mother and father. He missed his brother and sister, too.

It was too far for them to come to see him.

"But when summer is over, maybe I can go to see them before I start to school," he thought.

When he thought about the end of summer, he felt better.

VII RAIN

Crook Nose and Eagle Feather had built a new hogan. It was near the old one, and it was made of poles with brush laid across them. The old hogan, made of logs and dirt, was too hot for summer. The new one was cool.

On summer evenings they ate supper in front of the brush hogan. Crook Nose and his wife and children ate first. Eagle Feather ate what was left.

Sometimes there was not much, and he went to bed hungry.

He told Round Woman, "I want more to eat."

"We are not rich people," said Round Woman, "and we have had no rain for a long time. If we have no rain, our corn and squashes will die. Our sheep and goats will have no water. And you want more to eat. Ha! You eat too much already!"

56

Eagle Feather wanted to say, "You and Crook Nose have all you want to eat. Your children have all they want." But he did not say it.

He said to himself, "Summer will soon be over. Then I can go away from here."

One evening they were sitting in front of the new hogan.

Crook Nose asked Eagle Feather, "How much water is in the water hole?"

"Enough for one more day," said Eagle Feather. "Maybe two."

"Our sheep and goats will die without water," said Round Woman.

"It may rain soon," said Crook Nose. "There is a smell of rain in the air."

Eagle Feather did not think it would rain soon. He could smell no rain in the air.

But that night he awoke and heard thunder. It

was loud thunder, like someone beating on a drum.

Eagle Feather sat up. Through the sides of the brush hogan he could see lightning.

All at once, the rain began to pour. It poured into the brush hogan.

"Rain!" shouted Eagle Feather.

He and Crook Nose jumped up. They picked up all the blankets and sheepskins they could carry. Round Woman picked up the baby.

Small Boy began to cry. He was afraid of the thunder.

"I hear the devils!" he cried. "Don't let the devils get me!"

Round Woman took him by the hand. They all ran out through the rain and into the old hogan.

It was dry in the old hogan. Round Woman lit a fire to dry the sheepskins and blankets.

The baby was already asleep, tied to her cradle board. But Small Boy was still afraid.

"You should be happy," said Round Woman. "The rain is good. It will fill the water hole for the sheep and goats. It will make the grass green."

"Don't be afraid," said Crook Nose. "Look. I will show you something."

He took a bowl and a feather. He made the feather stand up in the bowl and dance.

Small Boy forgot to be afraid. "See!" he said. "See the feather!"

Eagle Feather saw that strings were tied to the feather. Crook Nose was pulling the strings to make it move. But Small Boy thought the feather was really dancing.

Crook Nose let the feather fall into the bowl. "It has gone to sleep," he said. "Now you must go to sleep, too."

59

THE FEATHER DANCE

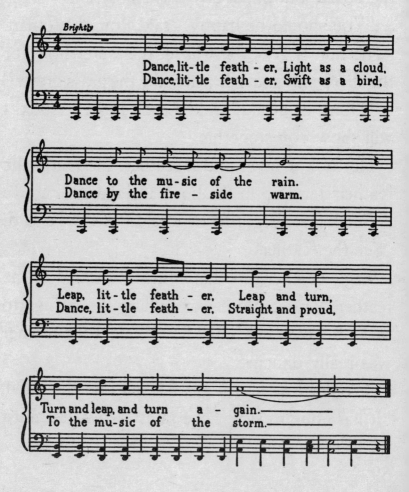

And Small Boy went to sleep.

After that rain, there were more. One rain came while Eagle Feather was out with the sheep and goats.

He knew a place under the rocks where he could be out of the rain. He drove the sheep and goats toward it. They ran into each other. They went running off through the bushes.

It took him a long time to drive them all under the rocks.

Then he saw a gray pony tied to a bush under the rocks. A boy was sitting by the bush. He was older than Eagle Feather.

For a while they looked at each other and said nothing.

The other boy spoke first. "It rains hard."

"Yes," said Eagle Feather. "My clothes are wet."

61

"Mine are dry," said the other boy. "I saw the rain coming. I rode in here before I got wet."

"Are you going far?" asked Eagle Feather.

"I am going home, over by the canyon," said the other boy. "I've been to town."

"My cousin Crook Nose said he would take me to town some day," said Eagle Feather, "but he never has."

"Do you live with Crook Nose?" asked the other boy.

"Yes. I work for him. But soon I am going to school."

"So am I," said the other boy. "Did you know school starts next week on Monday?"

"No," said Eagle Feather. "I'll tell my cousin Crook Nose tonight."

It was evening when the rain stopped. The other boy rode away. Eagle Feather drove the sheep and goats home.

Crook Nose was by the corral. Eagle Feather said to him, "A boy told me school will start next week on Monday."

Crook Nose said nothing.

63

"How will I get there?" asked Eagle Feather. "Will you take me in the truck?"

"Where?" asked Crook Nose.

"To school," said Eagle Feather.

"To school? You?" Crook Nose looked surprised. "You are working for me."

"You said if I worked all summer, I could go to school," said Eagle Feather.

"You didn't understand me," said Crook Nose. "You will have to work this winter, too. Next year we will talk about school."

"You said—" began Eagle Feather.

"You didn't understand me," said Crook Nose. He walked away.

"I *did* understand. And I won't work for you this winter. I've worked for you long enough!" said Eagle Feather.

But Crook Nose was too far away to hear him.

VIII THE COTTONWOOD TREE

That night Eagle Feather lay awake. He was waiting for the others to go to sleep. He had hidden his bow and arrows under a bush. He had hidden two pieces of bread inside his shirt. He was going to run away.

When he thought the others were asleep, he crawled out of the hogan.

A dry stick broke under his foot.

65

He began to run. There was a step behind him, and someone caught his arm.

It was Crook Nose.

"Where are you going?"

Eagle Feather tried to pull away. Crook Nose shook him.

"Where are you going?" he asked again.

"I want to go home," said Eagle Feather.

"This is your home," said Crook Nose.

"I want to go to my real home," said Eagle Feather.

"Don't try to run away again," said Crook Nose. "If you do, I'll strap you. I'll strap you, and I'll tie you up."

He pulled Eagle Feather back into the hogan.

Eagle Feather lay down. He lay for a long time with his eyes shut, but he was awake.

After a while Crook Nose began to snore.

66

Very softly Eagle Feather got to his hands and knees. Very softly he crawled out of the hogan. This time he made no noise.

He took his bow and arrows from under the bush where he had hidden them. He went running off through the sagebrush.

He was free! He was going home!

The moon was low in the sky. It did not give much light. He had to feel his way through the brush and over the rocks.

When daylight came, he was sleepy and tired. He did not know where he was, but he knew he had come a long way. He lay down under a big cottonwood tree and went to sleep.

He awoke suddenly. The sun was bright in his eyes.

He could hear a sound not far off. It was the sound of horses' hoofs.

Eagle Feather sat up and looked out through the brush. Two men on horseback were coming toward him. One of them he did not know. The other was Crook Nose.

They were looking down as they rode along. Eagle Feather knew they must have found his tracks in the soft earth.

He bent low and started to run through the brush. Then he saw that he was running toward a high rock cliff. The cliff was too steep to climb. He was trapped.

He lay flat on the ground. He tried to think what to do.

Crook Nose and the other man were so close he could hear them talking.

"His tracks go this way," said the other man.

"They go right to this big cottonwood tree," said Crook Nose.

"He may be hiding in the tree," said the other man.

Eagle Feather wished they *would* think he was hiding in the tree. As long as they looked in the tree, they would not know where he really was.

He looked through the bushes. The men were under the tree.

Eagle Feather put an arrow in his bow. He shot it into the tree.

"I heard something up there," said Crook Nose.

"So did I," said the other man.

The horses jumped as the arrow fell out of the tree.

"Look!" said Crook Nose. "One of his arrows!"

"He dropped it," said the other man. "He *is* up there."

"Come down!" called Crook Nose.

"Can you see him?" asked the other man.

"No. The leaves are too thick." Crook Nose called again, "Come down!"

"*I'll* bring him down." The other man got off his horse. He started to climb the cottonwood tree.

71

Eagle Feather saw the horse tied to a bush. He put his bow around his neck and his arrows inside his shirt. He lay flat on the ground and began to crawl.

He crawled to the bush where the man's horse was tied.

Crook Nose's back was turned. He was looking up into the tree.

Eagle Feather untied the horse. He jumped into the saddle.

Crook Nose turned and saw him. He gave a yell as Eagle Feather rode off through the brush.

Eagle Feather leaned forward in the saddle. The horse laid back its ears and ran.

Crook Nose was coming behind him. He was whipping his horse.

Eagle Feather saw the edge of the canyon ahead. He rode toward it.

Crook Nose was coming closer. His horse was bigger and faster.

"I've got you now!" he shouted.

Eagle Feather looked around. Crook Nose was coming up beside him.

Eagle Feather leaned far to one side and jumped. He landed in the middle of a bush.

Before Crook Nose could stop, Eagle Feather was on his feet. Straight for the canyon he ran. He slid down a steep bank. He jumped over a bush and slid down another bank.

No one on horseback could follow him here. Crook Nose could not find him among the rocks and trees of the canyon. Eagle Feather was safe.

IX THE LONG WALK

Deep in the canyon Eagle Feather sat down to rest. Inside his shirt he still had the two pieces of bread. He ate one of them.

He looked among the rocks for water. He had not had a drink for a long time.

Once he saw a man riding a horse up one of the canyon trails. The man had a water bottle tied to his saddle. Eagle Feather wanted to ask him for a drink, but he was afraid the man would try to take him back to Crook Nose. He hid until the man was gone.

All day he stayed in the canyon. He saw a snake lying on a log in the sun. He saw two young deer leaping and playing among the trees. He saw chipmunks running over the rocks. They were all afraid of him.

When it was night, he came out of the canyon. He looked all about him. He saw no one.

He began to walk toward home.

He did not like to be out alone after dark. He thought he could hear witches talking in the trees. Sometimes he thought the witches were after him, and he ran.

When the sun came up, he was glad. He knew the sun was his friend.

He ate the piece of bread he had left, and he was still hungry. He was thirsty, too.

But that day he had good luck. He followed a sheep trail and came to a water hole. He lay down and drank and drank.

Then he found an eagle feather among the rocks. It was like the one he had found when he was a baby.

He said to himself, "This will make me brave like an eagle."

He put the feather in his headband.

Eagle Feather walked all night. He felt braver than he had the night before.

All the next day he found no food or water. He looked for berries and pinyon nuts, but he could not find any. He tried to eat some leaves, but they were bitter and made him feel sick.

He walked that night until he was too tired to walk any farther. He went to sleep under a bush.

In the morning he looked about him. Now he knew where he was. There was a hill not far from home!

Soon he would be home!

He would see his mother and father. He would see Teasing Boy and Morning Bird. He would ride the spotted pony again.

He climbed the hill. He could see the corral. He could see the hogan.

He began to run.

"I'm home!" he shouted. "Look—I'm home!"

He ran to the door of the hogan. He stopped. Something was wrong. Everything was still. It was a stillness that made him afraid.

There were no horses tied near the hogan. There were no tracks in front of the door.

He called, "Mother? Father?"

There was no answer.

He looked into the hogan. No one was there. Everything was gone—the sheepskins, the big kettle, the saddles. It was like an empty shell.

Someone spoke behind him. "They are not here."

He turned around. Crook Nose was standing there.

Eagle Feather did not try to run. He was too weak and tired. He stood and looked at Crook Nose.

"Where are they?" he asked.

"I don't know," said Crook Nose, "but you can see they have gone and left you." He laughed. "Did you think you could get away from me? I knew you would come here. I have been waiting."

He caught Eagle Feather's arm.

"Let me go," said Eagle Feather.

"No. I'm going to take you back." Crook Nose pulled him along to where the truck was hidden in the brush. "Get in!"

Eagle Feather got in. The feather fell out of his headband, and he put it inside his shirt.

Crook Nose started the truck. They were on their way.

X TWO HORSES

They drove slowly along the rocky road.

Crook Nose stopped at a well. "I'm going to put water in the truck." He got out, and Eagle Feather got out with him.

"Don't try to run away," Crook Nose told him.

"I want a drink." Eagle Feather drank from the water tank. He got back into the truck.

Crook Nose looked at him as they drove along. "Are you sick?"

"No," said Eagle Feather.

"You are tired, I know that, and your feet must be sore," said Crook Nose. "You see what happens when you try to run away."

Eagle Feather said nothing. He was thinking of Father and Mother and his brother and sister. Where had they gone? Would he ever see them again?

The long ride was over. Crook Nose stopped in front of his hogan.

There were two horses tied outside. One was a yellow horse. The other was a spotted pony.

Eagle Feather thought, "That looks like the pony I used to ride at home."

He looked again. It *was* his pony!

A man came out of the hogan.

Eagle Feather jumped out of the truck. "Father!" he cried.

"My son! Oh, I'm glad to see you again! Where have you been?" asked Father. "They told me you had run away."

"I went back home," said Eagle Feather, "and no one was there."

"I went after him and brought him home in my truck." Crook Nose smiled and tried to look pleasant. "I didn't want anything bad to happen to him."

Father said to Eagle Feather, "While you were running away, I was on my way here. Why did you run away?"

"I didn't like it here," said Eagle Feather.

"He doesn't know what he is saying," said Crook Nose. "We give him the best of everything."

"He doesn't look as if he has had the best of everything," said Father. "He looks thin and hungry."

"That is because he ran away. Now he is hungry and tired," said Crook Nose. "You can't take him with you. I need him to help me. Don't forget, you said he could work here for a year."

"No!" said Eagle Feather. "Just the summer."

"That is right," said Father. "Just the summer. He has already been away from home too long. I came to take him back."

"No," said Crook Nose. "I must have someone to help me here."

"You are going back with me," Father said to Eagle Feather. "I brought the pony for you to ride. Listen. I have something to tell you. Do you remember Jimmie Redhorse, the man who worked at the trading post?"

"Yes," said Eagle Feather.

"He is going away to be a soldier. I am going to take his place and work at the trading post. We are living there now—your mother and brother and sister and I. We have a hogan back of the trading post. You are going to live with us and go to school."

85

"I can go to school and still be with you!" said Eagle Feather.

"School will do him no good," said Crook Nose. "Leave him with me. I will teach him all he needs to know."

"You had better teach yourself first," said Father. "Come, my son."

He got on the yellow horse. Eagle Feather got on the spotted pony. He felt something inside his shirt. He remembered the feather. He took it out and put it in his headband.

"I brought you this from the trading post," said Father. He held out a box of raisins.

Eagle Feather took the raisins. He knew Crook Nose and Round Woman were outside the hogan, watching him go, but he did not look back. He sat very straight in his saddle. He began to sing as he rode away beside his father.

IN THE SUMMER TIME

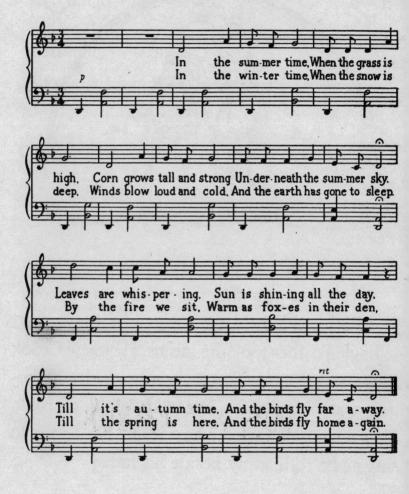